MINI RABBIT
Must Help

FOR
MUM
x

First published in hardback by HarperCollins *Children's Books* in 2020

3 5 7 9 10 8 6 4 2

HB ISBN: 978–0–00–826488–8
PB ISBN: 978–0–00–826489–5

HarperCollins *Children's Books* is a division of HarperCollins*Publishers* Ltd.

Text and illustrations copyright © John Bond 2020

Visit our website at: www.harpercollins.co.uk

Printed in Italy

MINI RABBIT
Must Help

JOHN BOND

HarperCollins *Children's Books*

Mother Rabbit is writing a
very important letter.

Can I HELP?

Can I post the letter?
CAN I?

I will be VERY careful.

Well, okay then, Mini Rabbit. But . . .

. . . the last collection is at
five o'clock, so hurry
and don't be LATE.

Oh no. I WON'T
be late.

Looks like Mini Rabbit needs to
pack a few things first.

Cake . . .

Slime . . .

Stick . . .

Mini Rabbit, do you REALLY need all those things?
You're going to be late.

I WON'T be late!
And I will be very,
VERY careful.

The bus will be here any minute now.

I have a VERY
important letter to post.
I CAN'T be late.

The bus is always late.
I will walk instead.

TOWN
5

Oh, look, here comes the bus.

Must help.
VERY important letter to post.
CAN'T be late.

There goes the bus!

Oh.

Mini Rabbit has FINALLY arrived in town.
Not much time left to post his letter now . . .

I'm HERE!

I have a very important letter.

I'm being very helpful.

Now Mini Rabbit just needs to
find the postbox for his letter.

I'm hungry.

I need my snack.

Then I will post my

very important letter.

Ah. Cake time. Mini Rabbit likes cake.
And it looks like somebody else might want some too.

Scoff
Scoff
Scoff
There you go,
bird.

WHOOPS!

Oh no, my letter.

I'm sure that cake
will just rub off the
very important letter . . .

Catch that letter . . .

It is VERY important!

LOOK!
I caught it!

Mini Rabbit should
probably try to post that
important letter now.

I will just
dry it off.

I WON'T be late . . .

Must

help . . .

Very . . .

important . . .

letter . . .

Hmmmm. Mini Rabbit's very important letter
is really quite far away now.

Should be just
around here . . .

somewhere.

Excuse me.

Have you seen my letter?
It is VERY important.

Nope.
No letters here,
Mini Rabbit.

It looks like Mini Rabbit might have lost
the letter, and it was VERY important.

But I was being
SO careful . . .

Oh dear. Mini Rabbit is going to have to tell
Mother Rabbit that he's LOST the
very important letter.

After all that, it looks like Mini Rabbit is too small to post the very important letter.

Hmmmm.
I know . . .

Sticky
SLIME!

There!

Well, that's one way
to post a letter.

Now Mini Rabbit can finally get the bus home.

Off it goes.

Goodbye, Mini Rabbit.

Oh, wait . . .

You—

Bye!
Thank you!

Mother Rabbit looks very pleased to see Mini Rabbit.

I posted it!

I posted the VERY important letter.

I was VERY helpful.

Well done, Mini Rabbit.